little
Suddenly!

First published in Great Britain by Andersen Press Ltd in 2000
First published in paperback by Collins Picture Books in 2002

1 3 5 7 9 10 8 6 4 2

ISBN 0-00-713235-2

Collins Picture Books is an imprint of the Children's Division, part of HarperCollins Publishers Ltd.
Text and illustrations copyright © Colin McNaughton 2000, 2002

The author/illustrator asserts the moral right
to be identified as the author/illustrator of the work.
A CIP catalogue record for this title is available from the British Library.

The HarperCollins website address is: www.fireandwater.com

Printed and bound in Hong Kong

little
Suddenly!

Colin McNaughton

Collins

An imprint of HarperCollinsPublishers

Preston! Someone's following you!

Look out Preston!

Careful Preston!

He's behind you Preston!

Preston!

Suddenly!

Preston is home.

Mister Wolf has bumped his head.

Preston Pig
is safe in bed.

Colin McNaughton is one of Britain's most highly-acclaimed picture book talents and a winner of many prestigious awards. His Preston Pig Stories are hugely successful with Preston now starring in his own animated television series on CITV.

Collect all the hilarious Preston Pig Stories:

little **Oops!**	little **Goal!**	little **Suddenly!**	little **BOO!**	**Shh!** (Don't Tell Mister Wolf)
0-00-713236-0	0-00-713234-4	0-00-713235-2	0-00-713237-9	0-00-664715-4

Suddenly!	**BOO!**	**Oops!**	**GOAL!**	**Hmm...**	**OompH!**
0-00-714013-4	0-00-714014-2	0-00-714015-0	0-00-714011-8	0-00-714012-6	0-00-712635-2

WHEE!	**POOH!**	**PARP!**
0-00-712371-X	0-00-712370-1	0-00-712372-8

"For sheer fun and verve, Colin McNaughton is unbeatable." Radio Times